# Lion's L[...]

### by Liza Charlesworth

ISBN: 978-1-338-78269-1
Illustrated by Michael Robertson
Copyright © 2021 by Liza Charlesworth. All rights reserved.
Published by Scholastic Inc., 557 Broadway, New York, NY 10012

10 9 8 7 6 5 4 3 2 1    68    21 22 23 24 25 26 27/0

Printed in Jiaxing, China. First printing, June 2021.

# ■SCHOLASTIC

Lion **had** a pizza.
Yummy, yummy!

2

Lion **had** a salad.
Yummy, yummy!

3

Lion **had** a sandwich.
Yummy, yummy!

4

Lion **had** a watermelon.
Yummy, yummy!

Lion **had** a taco.
Yummy, yummy!

Lion **had** a cake.
Yummy, Yummy!

Lion **had** a tummy-ache.
Yucky, yucky!